AF228518

GIRLS' GYMNASTICS

By Brendan Flynn

An Imprint of Abdo Publishing
abdobooks.com

abdobooks.com

Published by Abdo Publishing, a division of ABDO, PO Box 398166, Minneapolis, Minnesota 55439. Copyright © 2022 by Abdo Consulting Group, Inc. International copyrights reserved in all countries. No part of this book may be reproduced in any form without written permission from the publisher. SportsZone™ is a trademark and logo of Abdo Publishing.

Printed in the United States of America, North Mankato, Minnesota.
102021
012022

Cover Photo: Victoria Viar Pro/Shutterstock Images
Interior Photos: Dmitri Lovetski/AP Images, 4–5, 9; Laurence Griffiths/Getty Images Sport/Getty Images, 7, 34; Wei Zheng/ChinaSports/Visual China Group/Getty Images, 10; Ezra Shaw/Getty Images Sport/Getty Images, 12–13; Lars Baron/Getty Images Sport/Getty Images, 15; Xinhua/Imago/Icon Sportswire, 17; Tim Clayton/Corbis Sport/Getty Images, 19; Marijan Murat/picture alliance/Getty Images, 20–21; Maja Hitij/Getty Images Sport/Getty Images, 23; Jeff Roberson/AP Images, 25; Marijan Murat/picture-alliance/dpa/AP Images, 26; Ashley Landis/AP Images, 28–29, 33, 43; Natacha Pisarenko/AP Images, 31; Kyodo/AP Images, 36–37; Grigory Syosev/Sputnik/AP Images, 39; Cheng Min/Xinhua News Agency/Getty Images, 41; Red Line Editorial, 44

Editor: Charlie Beattie
Series Designer: Jake Nordby

Library of Congress Control Number: 2021941597

Publisher's Cataloging-in-Publication Data

Names: Flynn, Brendan, author.
Title: Girls' Gymnastics / by Brendan Flynn
Description: Minneapolis, Minnesota : Abdo Publishing, 2022 | Series: Girls' SportsZone | Includes online resources and index.
Identifiers: ISBN 9781532196348 (lib. bdg.) | ISBN 9781098218157 (ebook)
Subjects: LCSH: Gymnastics--Juvenile literature. | Sports for girls--Juvenile literature. | Gymnastics for girls--Juvenile literature. | Team sports--Juvenile literature.
Classification: DDC 796.44--dc23

TABLE OF CONTENTS

POWER AND GRACE WITH SIMONE BILES

Simone Biles seems to make history every time she competes. But she topped herself at the 2019 World Championships in Stuttgart, Germany.

Biles won an incredible five gold medals that week. Along with her US teammates, she took the top spot in the team competition. Biles then won her fifth all-around world title. Finally, she topped the individual fields in balance beam, floor exercise, and vault.

Biles went even further to demonstrate her greatness. In gymnastics, athletes can get skills named after them. They just need to be the first to successfully perform the skill in a major competition. In Stuttgart, Biles debuted two new skills. This made a total of four skills now called the Biles.

On the balance beam, Biles broke out a double-twisting, double-backflip dismount. In the floor exercise, Biles landed a triple-twisting double backflip. The new floor skill is called the

Simone Biles salutes at the end of her vault during the all-around competition at the 2016 Olympic Games in Rio de Janeiro, Brazil.

Biles II. That's because she already had a skill named for her on floor. It was a double layout with a half twist.

A Note on Judging

Beginning in 2006, judges began giving not one but two scores for each routine. The difficulty score measures the hardness of the skills in the routine. It is sometimes called the D-score or start value. Gymnasts get extra points for doing difficult moves in combination with one another. The execution score (E-score) is based on form. A separate panel of judges calculates this score. Execution judges start from 10 points and deduct tenths of a point for form errors. At the end of a routine, the D-score is added to the E-score for the total score on the event.

"She is, without question, the most dominant gymnast in the history of the sport," said two-time Olympic gold medalist Bart Conner. "She's doing the most difficult gymnastics ever attempted, and she does it effortlessly." But what makes her so great? It's a combination of qualities, but it boils down to two traits that elite gymnasts must have: power and grace.

Packing a Punch

When you're just 4 feet, 8 inches tall, it can be hard to stand out in a crowd. But Biles uses her short stature to her advantage. Because she's shorter, it is easier for her complete a rotation in the air. She's also incredibly consistent with her movements. Her arm and leg positions are precise when she's whirling through the air.

Biles flips above the balance beam while performing at the 2020 Olympic Games in Tokyo, Japan.

Biles's incredible strength gives her the time and speed needed to complete her skills. Her powerful body allows her to push higher off the vault and reach great heights on her tumbling passes. That maximizes her time in the air. Then she has more time to perform twists and flips on her dismount. Biles also has excellent balance, allowing her to move smoothly and confidently on the balance beam.

"What sets her apart is her strength, balance, coordination, and muscle control that produce faster rotation rates once she's in the air," said Dr. David Young, a physics professor at Louisiana State University. "Of course, she then needs the skill, timing, and training to know when to unwind all that rotational energy and stick the landing."

Grace Under Pressure

Gymnastics is not just about power and speed. Artistry is another important element. Performers must show a graceful mastery of their skills. Judges watch for a routine executed with style.

Dance movements add an artistic touch to the athletic demonstrations of tumbling and twisting. Judges look for

QUICK TIP:
STRENGTH BUILDERS

A gymnast looking to become more powerful on vault and floor exercise should work on increasing her strength. Nastia Liukin was tall and lanky compared to other gymnasts. She knew she had to get stronger to become elite. "I never had to work as hard on flexibility and dance as I did on strength," she said. "I remember to this day spending hours and hours a day conditioning in the gym and running up hills and sprints and jumps and all these things. And that's something that to a lot of the other gymnasts is second nature."

gymnasts to show good form in both areas. Examples of good form include straight legs, pointed toes, and correct technique on gymnastic movements. Gymnasts also try to make difficult routines look easy to do. "We really put a lot of time and effort, a lot of hard work into it to make it look really easy," said 2008 Olympic gold medalist Nastia Liukin.

Biles congratulates gold medalist Guan Chenchen of China after the balance beam final at the 2020 Olympics. Biles won the bronze medal in the event.

One way to encourage good form in gymnastics is to practice ballet. Many gymnasts study ballet in addition to regular training. It helps with flexibility. Ballet classes also help gymnasts polish dance skills and refine their movements. That can lead to higher execution scores.

Biles found another way to demonstrate power and grace at the Tokyo Olympics in July 2021. Biles lost track of where she was in the air during a vault. When this happens for a gymnast, competing can be very dangerous. So she pulled herself out of the team competition. The condition she was experiencing is what gymnasts call the "twisties."

Biles was in the brightest spotlight of her career. But she was able to step back when she knew she was putting herself in danger. The decision also gave others a chance to compete. While she was sidelined, Biles offered cheers, tips, and support to her teammates. She was able to return to compete in the individual balance beam competition, where she won a bronze medal.

What Are the Twisties?

Gymnasts rely on muscle memory gained through years of practice when they perform their skills. That means they aren't thinking about all the different flips and twists they must make in midair. Their brains and bodies work together to complete the motions automatically. But sometimes, that connection isn't working right. Gymnasts call this the twisties, and it can happen for many reasons and at any time. When Biles experienced this dangerous condition at the Tokyo Olympics in 2021, she decided to sit out until she knew it was safe to compete again. A gymnast who loses that mind-body connection in the middle of a routine could land awkwardly and suffer serious injury. Biles knew that no medal was worth that type of risk.

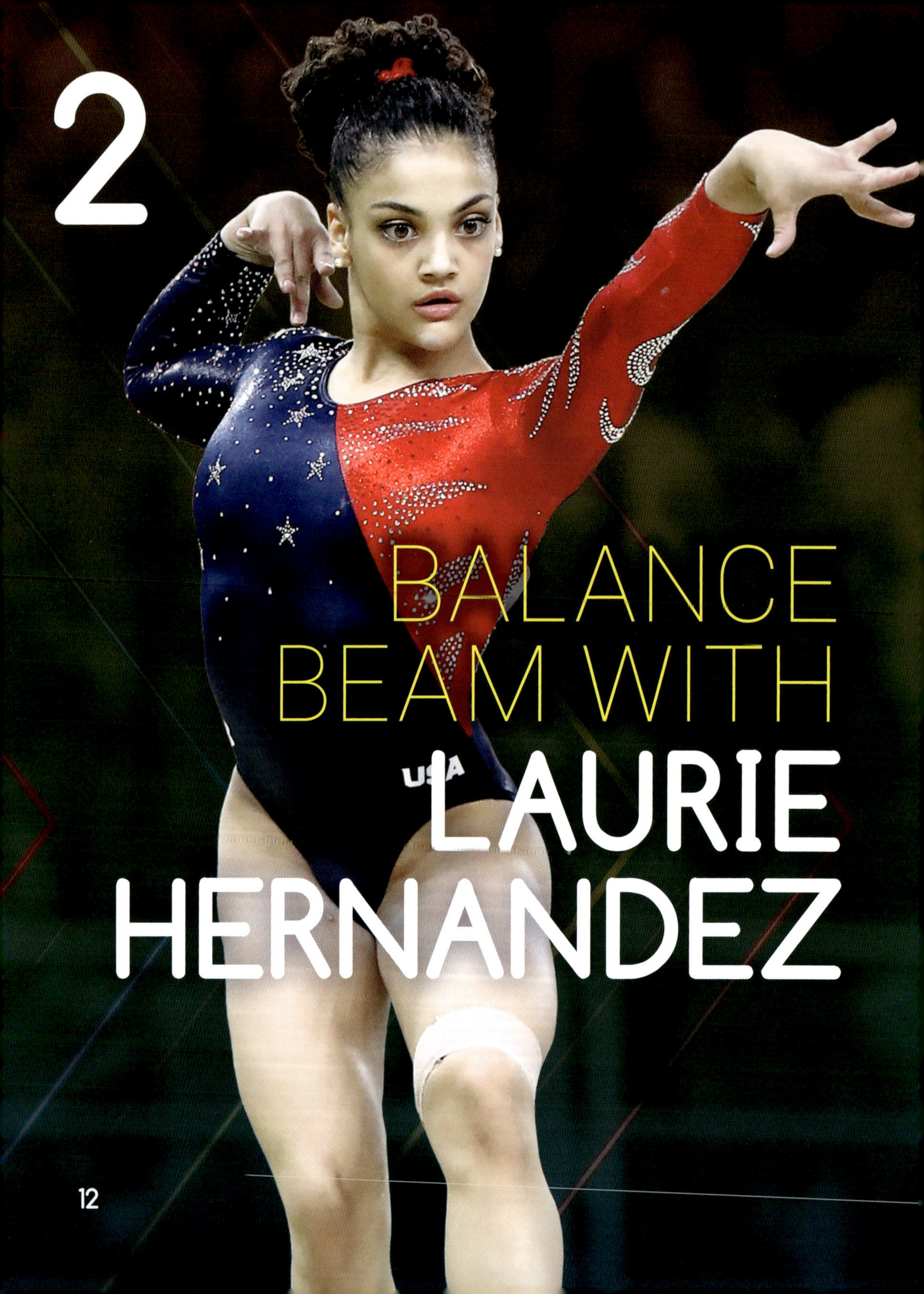

2

BALANCE BEAM WITH LAURIE HERNANDEZ

The world's top athletes met in Rio de Janeiro, Brazil, for the 2016 Olympic Games. The members of the US women's gymnastics team were strong contenders to win their second straight gold in the team competition. They won it easily. Now the US women were looking for a strong showing in the individual event finals.

Simone Biles was in the middle of dominating the sport. She had already won three golds in Rio, and she was expected to add another in the balance beam. Biles had qualified with the top score of 15.633. Her 16-year-old teammate Laurie Hernandez wasn't far behind. Hernandez posted the second-highest qualifying score at 15.366. A year earlier, the idea of Biles and Hernandez finishing one-two in the event would have been unthinkable. Hernandez was still competing at the junior level. But she moved through the ranks quickly in her first year as a senior. Hernandez placed third in the all-around at nationals. Then she was second in the

Laurie Hernandez knew the balance beam might be her best shot for an individual medal at the 2016 Olympics in Rio de Janeiro, Brazil.

all-around at the Olympic Trials, where she posted the top score on beam.

With her bubbly personality and expressive eyes, Hernandez was known as the "human emoji." A gymnast's enthusiasm and emotion can have a positive influence on judges. But few people assumed the youngest member of the team would have a chance to surpass Biles in the finals.

Conquering Fear

There is little room for error on the balance beam. As such, many gymnasts think beam is the most nerve-racking event. Jordyn Wieber, who starred for Team USA in the 2012 London Olympics, dealt with the pressure by visualizing a perfect routine. She also reminded herself of all the preparation she had done. "I call it getting into my zone before the competition," Wieber said. "A lot of times I'm just running through my keywords in my head, all the keywords that I practice in my head in the gym every single day, just making it feel totally normal."

Biles performed third of the eight gymnasts seeking gold in the beam. Her routine had a high degree of difficulty. It would be nearly impossible to beat if her performance was clean.

Biles got off to a strong start. But midway through her 90-second routine, she slipped while trying to land a somersault. Biles grabbed the beam to steady herself. That calls for an automatic 0.5-point deduction from a final score.

Hernandez flips during her silver medal–winning routine at the 2016 Games.

Biles's final score of 14.733 left the door open for her competitors. It didn't take long for one to pass her. Sanne Wevers of the Netherlands was up next. She posted a 15.466 to surge into first place with four gymnasts left to go.

Hernandez went sixth. Before she approached the beam, she got a bit of support from one of her teammates. "You got this. Just stay calm," Biles whispered to Hernandez.

Just before she leaped onto the beam, the TV cameras caught Hernandez repeating it to herself one last time: "I got this." Hernandez opened simply with a front pike. Her routine quickly became more complex. Most gymnasts prefer to do their toughest skills at the beginning of their beam routines. That way, they get the difficulty out of the way early.

Hernandez worked her way back across the beam with an aerial followed by a split leap. That set up a combination of skills—a backward walkover and a double layout. She completed them with just the slightest wobble.

Hernandez's confidence was growing, but she stayed focused and charged on. Her leaps and spins grew more fluid and precise. She completed the routine with a flawless double-pike dismount. Hernandez threw her arms into the air with excitement. Congratulations awaited her as she

Speaking Up

Laurie Hernandez didn't qualify for the 2020 Tokyo Games. But she still made a big impact on the sport and her fellow gymnasts. Hernandez said she'd suffered years of verbal and emotional abuse from her longtime coach. The coach was investigated and eventually suspended by USA Gymnastics as a result. Hernandez encouraged other gymnasts to speak openly if adults are mistreating them. She also told athletes to be conscious of their own mental health needs amid the difficulties of competition.

Hernandez, *right*, and Simone Biles pose with their medals after taking silver and bronze in the 2016 Olympic balance beam final.

returned to the sidelines. The crowd roared as they awaited the results posted by the judges. Finally, the scoreboard flashed. Hernandez had come up just short of Wevers with a 15.333. But she wasn't too disappointed. After all, she had performed her best on the world's biggest stage.

"I think this is one of the best routines that I've showed in Rio," Hernandez said afterward. "I'm just happy I could perform the way I do in practice and stay calm through the whole thing."

Finding a Balance on Beam

More than any other event, balance beam makes gymnasts nervous. The smallest mistake can lead to a fall. A gymnast must be careful when simply walking across the beam. Imagine landing, flipping, and turning on the four-inch (10-cm) plank. Then try making it look perfectly natural. That's just what the most advanced gymnasts do.

A salto element is a move where a gymnast does a flip without touching her hands to the ground (or in this case, to the beam). Top-level gymnasts are required to have a combination of at least two flipping elements in their beam routines. This is called a "flight series." The gymnast uses the first flip to build momentum for a second and possibly a third salto.

QUICK TIP:
START ON A LINE

Even after learning a salto, gymnasts need a lot of practice before they can do it on the high beam. One accomplished coach who has worked with many US national team athletes suggests progressing gradually. Start by working the flip on a line on the floor and pretending you're doing it on the beam. Then move to a practice beam a few inches off the ground. Practice doing the skill onto a pile of mats raised up beam-high with a line drawn on it to simulate the end of the beam.

Confidence was key for Hernandez during the 2016 Olympic balance beam final.

Balance beam is about taking risks. Nothing is riskier than flipping upside down without using your hands. It takes incredible precision to turn your body over in the air and stick the landing on a narrow plank, let alone make it look easy.

Front or back handsprings often set up salto elements. A gymnast may land the flip one foot at a time. This is called a walkout. Others choose to land with both feet at the same time on the beam. As with release moves on bars, judges look for good form on salto elements, including pointed toes and straight legs.

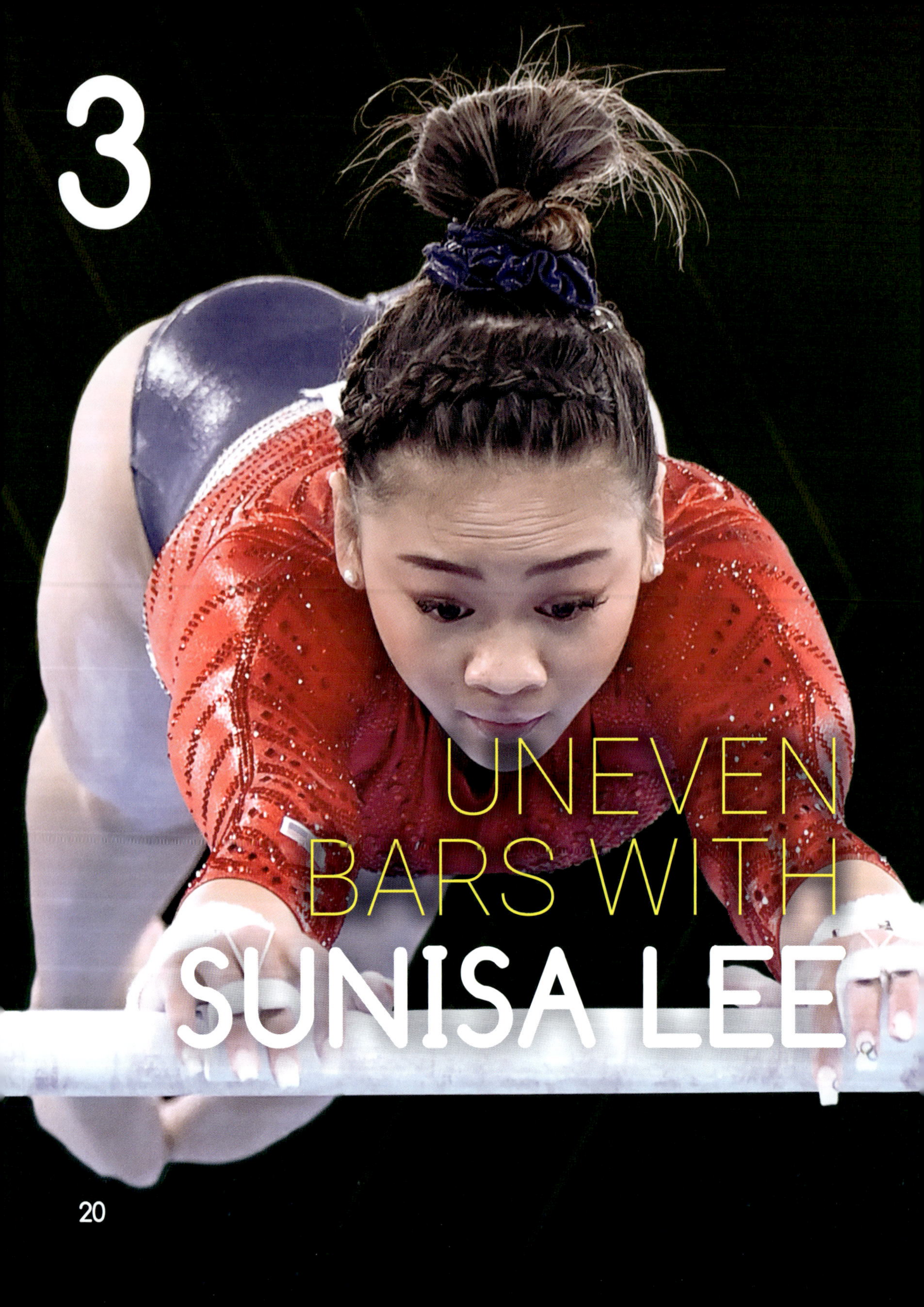

3

UNEVEN BARS WITH SUNISA LEE

Regardless of the outcome, the 2021 US National Championships were guaranteed to be a special event for Sunisa Lee. Lee, from St. Paul, Minnesota, comes from a tight-knit family. She is of Hmong descent. The Hmong people live in several countries in southeast Asia, including Laos, where Lee's parents were born. With a strong performance at nationals and then the Olympic trials, Lee could become the first US Olympian of Hmong descent. Heritage and family are important to Lee. She said she knows her success "means a lot to the Hmong community . . . and to just be an inspiration to other Hmong people [means] a lot to me too."

But the road to the competition was not smooth. In August 2019, Lee's father, John, fell off a ladder while helping a neighbor trim a tree. The accident left him paralyzed from the chest down.

Then in 2020, the COVID-19 pandemic shut down the sporting world and delayed the upcoming Tokyo Olympic Games. Lee also lost an aunt and an uncle to the virus. Then, when Lee resumed training that summer, she suffered an ankle injury that limited her training for months.

Not Just for the Short Gymnasts

Looking back on the ordeal, Lee was able to see the positive rather than focus on the negative. "It's helped because it makes me want this even more," she said. "I want to do it for my family and coaches obviously, but I also want to do it for myself. I've just been through so much."

So, when Lee entered the US Nationals arena in Fort Worth, Texas, in early June 2021, the 18-year-old was determined to put on a show Just before her routine on the uneven bars, she spotted her parents in the crowd. That was all the inspiration she needed to put together a winning performance.

Lee performed one of the most difficult uneven bars routines at the Tokyo Olympics.

Lee is known for having one of the most difficult bar routines in the world. She put all her skills on display that night. She started with a Nabieva—a release move in which the gymnast swings around the high bar before grabbing the bar again.

She then connected that skill to a Bhardwaj. That's a layout salto with a full twist to the low bar. After that perfect transition, she was on a roll. She confidently cruised through her routine. Lee nailed each release move and twisted through the air with fluidity and grace. At the end, she built up speed for her dismount with three full rotations around the high bar. She then stuck the landing as the crowd erupted.

Lee scored a 15.300 on that routine—6.800 for difficulty and 8.500 for execution. It was by far the highest score of the day. Simone Biles came in second at 14.750. Lee went on to post the same score on the same routine at the US Olympic Trials. It helped her earn a spot on Team USA for the Tokyo Olympic Games.

In Tokyo, Lee won a gold medal, but not the one most expected her to win. She made an uncharacteristic error in the uneven bars final and ended up with the bronze. But Lee surprised everyone and won gold in the all-around. Another 15.300 on the bars set her up for the victory in the all-around competition.

Mastering the Bars

The uneven bars is one of the most technical events in women's gymnastics. It takes precision and strength—and a lot of hard work—to master the basics. Once those have been

learned, a gymnast can move on to more complicated skills, including release moves.

The Nabieva that Lee performed is one of the more difficult release moves. It is a form of a Tkatchev. The skill requires the gymnast to release the bar and soar backward and over it. She then regrasps the bar when it is about level with her chest. The Tkatchev can be done in a variety of ways. Most gymnasts learn a regular Tkatchev. That is when they swing their legs into a straddle position as they go over the bar. It's also possible to do a Tkatchev in a piked position. That is where the gymnast bends at the hips but keeps her legs glued together.

Lee flips over the bar while performing a Nabieva.

There are even more advanced versions of the Tkatchev. In one, a gymnast will swing into the skill with both her hands and toes on the bar. Using her legs and feet, she'll push off the bar to get more height and flight as she flies over it. These "toe on" skills are riskier and more difficult. But they nearly always draw roars of approval from the crowd. The Nabieva that Lee performed was a "toe on" skill. Lee then traveled back over the bar in a layout position. The Tkatchev is one of the most popular skills on uneven bars. What separates good from great Tkatchevs is the amount of height a gymnast gets when performing the skill. Great height on Tkatchevs can make the judges sit up and take note. And having good form is key too. That means the gymnast's legs should be straight and her toes pointed.

That said, release moves are not for beginners. In fact, learning a release skill on bars is seen as a rite of passage into very advanced gymnastics. Asked about her proudest moment in gymnastics, two-time Olympic gold medalist Shannon Miller said: "Learning my first release move ranks right up there."

QUICK TIP:
SWING, SWING

Gymnasts practice a great deal before learning release moves. Coach Al Fong has a good way for gymnasts to prepare. He suggests the gymnast practice swinging from the high bar to the low bar while trying not to touch their feet on the ground. That way, the gymnast gets used to releasing a bar and catching it again without doing anything too complicated. Later, a gymnast might change to a backward swinging motion on high bar, let go of the bar, and fly over the low bar, trying to catch the low bar as she comes down.

4

VAULT WITH MYKAYLA SKINNER

MyKayla Skinner wasn't even supposed to be in the vault finals at the Tokyo Olympic Games in 2021. Then again, she was used to making comebacks.

Skinner took bronze on the vault at the 2014 world championships. She was later selected to go to the 2016 Rio de Janeiro Olympics as an alternate for Team USA, meaning she could only participate if someone got injured. Skinner did not end up competing in the Games. Afterward, she began her collegiate career at the University of Utah. Most fans assumed her days as an elite gymnast were over.

But in 2019 she announced she was returning. Skinner wanted to take one last shot at becoming an Olympian. The Tokyo Olympics were scheduled for the summer of 2020. Instead, due to the COVID-19 pandemic, they were pushed back a year. Then in January 2021, Skinner contracted pneumonia after becoming ill with COVID-19. The setback forced the 24-year-old Arizonan to take a break from training. That put her chances to earn a spot on Team USA in doubt. Instead, Skinner came back with some of her best routines ever at the Olympic Trials. That was enough to secure her spot in Tokyo as an individual.

Backward

To most people, the idea of going onto the vault table backward seems crazy. Soviet gymnast Natalia Yurchenko was not one of them. She competed during the early 1980s. Before then, gymnasts launched themselves at the vault while facing forward. Yurchenko used a roundoff onto the springboard. It gave her incredible backward momentum. That allowed her to flip and twist more easily off the vault. It was not long before gymnasts all over the world were learning the Yurchenko. Today it is the base for the Amanar and many other vaults.

The vault was Skinner's best event. During the qualifying round in Tokyo, Skinner posted a score of 14.866. That was the fourth-best score on the vault that day. Normally that would have been enough to send her to the eight-person finals. However, fellow Americans Simone Biles and Jade Carey were first and second. Olympic rules state that only two gymnasts per country can advance to each final. Skinner's Olympics appeared to be over. "I kind of had my mindset like, I'm done and ready to move on," Skinner said. She was preparing to catch a flight back to the United States when her world changed. Biles had pulled out of the team all-around finals.

She later pulled out of the vault final as well, giving Skinner a second shot at winning a medal.

Skinner was the first of the eight gymnasts to compete in the vault final. She opened with a difficult vault called a Cheng. The gymnast starts with a roundoff to back handspring, then does a half-twist onto the vault table. That leads to a 1.5-twist layout. Skinner nailed everything but the landing, which included a slight hop backward. The judges awarded her a score of 15.033. Her second attempt was an Amanar—another difficult vault. It also begins with a roundoff back handspring. Then the gymnast performs a back layout with 2.5 twists. Skinner had solid form but a wobbly landing. Her score of

14.800 gave her a two-vault average of 14.916. That ended up being good enough for the silver medal behind Brazil's Rebecca Andrade.

"This seriously means so much," Skinner said. "After having COVID, I seriously didn't know I would be able to go back into the gym, so just being able to overcome that and to keep pushing for my goals and dreams to make it to the Olympics has been such an honor. And now to even be in for [the] vault [final] and to win a silver medal, that's icing on the cake for me. Seriously, so unreal."

Why an Amanar?

The Amanar vault is named after Romanian gymnast Simona Amanar. She was the gold medalist on vault from the 1996 Olympic Games. Her final competition was at the 2000 Games. There she became the first woman to do a Yurchenko vault with two and a half twists. Amanar did not do the risky vault very well. It probably cost her a medal in the event. All the same, it landed her in gymnastics history books. That is because she was the first to perform the skill at a major event, so it took her name.

Vaulting to Success

The Amanar and Cheng vaults are two of the most difficult skills in women's gymnastics. The gymnasts who can do them receive a higher degree of difficulty score than most other vaults. That gives those gymnasts—and their teams—a big advantage.

Vaulting is the quickest event in women's gymnastics.

From beginning to end, a gymnast's vault lasts less than 10 seconds. But a lot happens in that time.

The gymnast starts at the end of the vaulting runway and runs toward the table, hitting the springboard with full force. That lifts her into the air and helps propel her over the table. During the second part of the vault, she flies away from the table and lands on her feet.

At 24 years old, Skinner was the oldest gymnast to compete for the United States since the 2004 Olympics.

Beginners start by learning simple vaults. As they progress, they might add an extra flip or twist. The most complicated vaults, like Skinner's Amanar and Cheng, involve multiple flips and a lot of twisting.

In most competitions, gymnasts do one vault. But in the event finals at major meets, gymnasts are required to show two different vaults to prove how they've mastered the event.

Form is very important while vaulting. Judges look for a clean, tight twist. The legs should be straight. The knees should be together and the toes pointed. Properly executing an Amanar is especially difficult. The gymnast should be completely extended while flying through the air, not bent or piked at the waist.

A good "block," or push, off the vaulting table is important to any vault. This is how a gymnast gets enough height to complete the skill. It is particularly key for the Amanar. To get a good block off the table, the gymnast must position her back handspring entry at just the right angle.

QUICK TIP:
YURCHENKO PROGRESSIONS

No gymnast, even one as talented as MyKayla Skinner, starts out doing Amanars and Chengs. First, they need to get comfortable. After all, they must approach the vaulting table while flying backward and upside down. It's not easy. One exercise is to work a roundoff back handspring and back tucks onto an eight-inch (20-cm) mat. Your feet should land just in front of the mat and force you to lift a little higher to get your hands onto the mat to complete the back handspring. As you grow more comfortable with this, an additional eight-inch mat can be added. This increases the height of the obstacle to simulate the vaulting table.

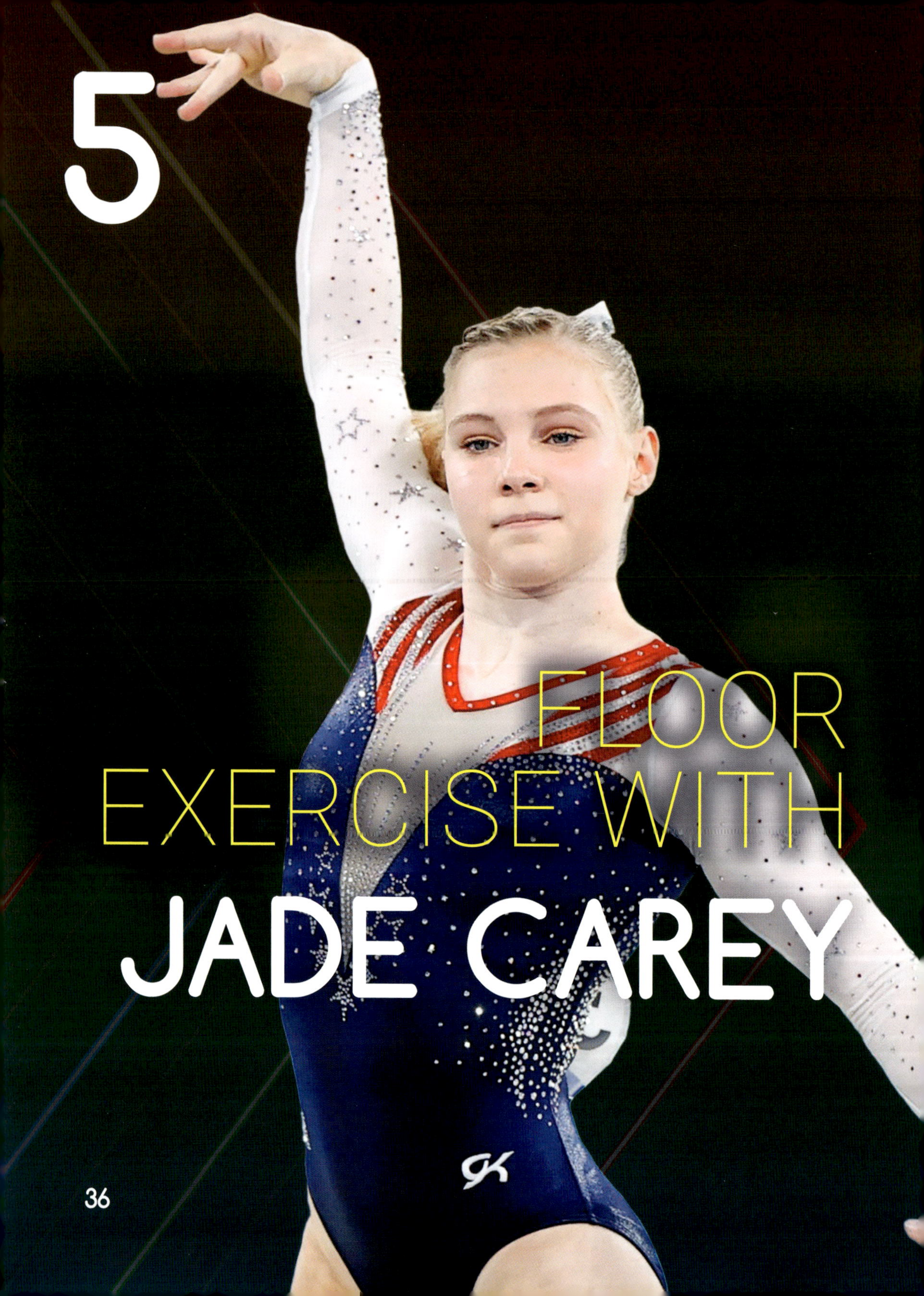

5

FLOOR EXERCISE WITH JADE CAREY

A lot can change in 24 hours. Just ask
Jade Carey. She shows strength in all four
disciplines, but she's at her best on vault and
floor exercise. So, when the 21-year-old
Carey showed up for the vault finals at
the Ariake Gymnastics Centre in Tokyo on
August 1, 2021, Olympic expectations ran high
for the Arizona native.

Then disaster struck. Carey lost track of
her steps as she made her approach for her
first attempt. She had planned on performing a
difficult vault. Instead, the stumble forced her
to bail out and settle for a simpler vault. It had
a much lower degree of difficulty.

A hush fell over the shocked crowd as they
realized what had happened. Carey's blunder
cost her any chance of a medal.

But Carey didn't have much time to feel
sorry for herself. She had also qualified for the
final in the floor exercise scheduled for the next
day. Fortunately, her father, Brian—who is also

Jade Carey lived up to her reputation as one of the
world's best on floor exercise at the 2020 Olympic
Games in Tokyo, Japan.

her coach—was there to give her some important advice the next morning.

"You might feel like yesterday was one of the worst days of your life," he told her. "But today can be one of the best days of your life. So just don't give up. Keep going."

We All Fall Down

Falling is a part of gymnastics. That is especially true when it comes to learning new skills. When asked the secret to her success, 2009 floor exercise world champion Beth Tweddle of Great Britain remarked, "It's just a lot of numbers and a lot of splatting before I get it correct."

Carey performed second on the floor in the final. She chose a song called "Powerful" by Ellie Goulding and Major Lazer as her music. The title was a perfect description of her performance.

Carey opened with a flawlessly executed double-twisting double layout on her first tumbling pass. Her face displayed calm confidence as she continued. Her tumbling and landings were strong. When Carey stuck her final landing, her teammates exploded into cheers. Carey hopped off the floor to hug her father.

Carey's routine was more difficult than those of her competitors. But that's not surprising. She's known for dynamic, challenging moves on the mat. She had been working on a

Carey's powerful and controlled tumbling helped her post a winning score of 14.366 in the Olympic floor exercise final.

triple-twisting, double-layout combination that no woman had ever landed in competition.

She didn't break out that move for the Olympic final, but she didn't need to. Her performance and degree of difficulty gave her a score of 14.366. "I've kind of been planning since qualifications that I was just going to do that because

I'm just so comfortable with that routine," she said of her decision-making process. "It's clean, and I know that I can do it." Carey had to sit through six other gymnasts doing their best to knock her off the top of the podium. None of them came close. The silver medalist, Vanessa Ferrari of Italy, scored a 14.200.

Later, Carey called her performance "the best floor routine I've ever done in my life." It came at the perfect time, just 24 hours after one of her biggest disappointments.

Different Doubles

The double back salto is the easiest form of double salto. Once a gymnast has mastered it, there are all kinds of complicated variations that can be learned. Double saltos can be done forward and backward. They can also be done in the tucked, piked, or layout (body completely stretched) positions. The layout is the hardest. Many top gymnasts also add twists to their double saltos. The most difficult variation ever done in competition is Simone Biles's triple-twisting double-tuck.

Fun on the Floor

The floor exercise is the only gymnastics event done to music, and it's often a fan favorite. To be good on floor, gymnasts must master a series of acrobatic elements. These can be put together to create tumbling passes. They also need to perform dance skills such as leaps and turns. Routines can be up to 90 seconds long, and a gymnast must perform the whole time.

Young gymnasts must master basic tumbling skills, including handsprings, walkovers, and simple saltos. Then they can begin practicing more difficult flips and twists. Salto skills are among the first advanced techniques gymnasts learn. Double saltos can be done both forward and backward, but they are most often done backward.

Because of their difficulty, double salto skills impress both the audience and judges. The gymnast who does several cleanly in her floor routine will usually earn a higher difficulty score than a gymnast who mainly relies on twisting elements when she tumbles.

A gymnast's legs should look like they are glued together for a good double salto. Sometimes the legs should be straight. Other times the straight legs should be tucked tight to the chest. This is if the skill is being done in the piked position.

QUICK TIP:
DOUBLING UP

Before a gymnast can safely perform a double salto skill, her body and mind must get used to the idea of flipping twice. Coach Al Fong has a nifty drill for gymnasts beginning to work double back saltos. The gymnast stands on a mat shaped like a cheese wedge, which is stacked on top of a larger mat in front of a trampoline. Standing on the cheese mat, the gymnast bounces onto the trampoline and rebounds backward. Then she performs a back flip with an extra quarter salto, landing on her back on the cheese. "I love this drill," says Canadian coach Rick McCharles. "It's safe, easy, fun, and encourages good technique."

Some gymnasts tend to do double saltos in "cowboy" position, with their legs apart. It allows for faster rotation and can help perform more difficult skills. However, in elite gymnastics competition it results in a deduction. Good toepoint is also a must, even when rotating at high-speed upside down.

DIAGRAM

BALANCE BEAM

The balance beam tests a gymnast's balancing abilities, but also her nerve. Just four inches (10 cm) wide and four feet (1.2 m) off the ground, it can feel much higher when a gymnast is standing on it and thinking about doing a flip!

VAULT

The Olympic vault runway is 82 feet (25 m) long and leads to a springboard in front of a leather-covered vaulting table. The vaulting table replaced the narrower vaulting "horse" in international competition in 2001.

FLOOR EXERCISE

The floor exercise mat is 40 feet (12.2 m) long and 40 feet wide, with springs underneath a carpeted surface, allowing gymnasts to get more height on their tumbling passes, leaps, and jumps. Women's floor exercise is performed to music.

UNEVEN BARS

No event has changed more over the years than uneven bars. The bars were once closer together, but today they are set wider apart, so the gymnast has more room to swing and do big skills.

GLOSSARY

acrobatic

Gymnastics moves such as handsprings and flips that are not dance elements.

block

The push off the vaulting table that launches the gymnast into the afterflight of her vault.

conditioning

Performing exercises such as pull-ups and push-ups that help a gymnast become stronger.

dismount

The last acrobatic move in a routine. On bars and beam, the gymnast dismounts off the apparatus and lands on a mat.

pike

A position where a gymnast keeps her legs straight but bends forward at the torso.

rotation

A twist or flip done while in the air.

salto

A flip completed without one's hands, done forward or backward.

straddle

A position where the gymnast points her legs in opposite directions as though she were doing middle splits.

stuck landing

When a gymnast lands a dismount or tumbling pass and doesn't have to move her feet.

tumbling/ tumbling pass

A sequence of acrobatic skills done on floor or beam involving handsprings, flips, and/or twists.

MORE INFORMATION

BOOKS

Lawrence, Blythe. *History of Gymnastics*. Minneapolis, MN: Abdo, 2021.

Nicks, Erin. *Guide to Competitive Gymnastics*. Minneapolis, MN: Abdo, 2021.

Rule, Heather. *All about Women's College Gymnastics*. Minneapolis, MN: Abdo, 2021.

ONLINE RESOURCES

To learn more about women's gymnastics, please visit **abdobooklinks.com** or scan this QR code. These links are routinely monitored and updated to provide the most current information available.

PLACES TO VISIT

International Gymnastics Hall of Fame

2020 Remington Place
Oklahoma City, OK 73111
405-602-6664
ighof.com

Located inside Science Museum Oklahoma, the International Gymnastics Hall of Fame honors those who have had amazing achievements within the sport or contributed to the sport's growth. The Hall of Fame features collections that show the history of the sport and highlight the best gymnasts through memorabilia, videos, and photos.

US Olympic & Paralympic Training Center

One Olympic Plaza
Colorado Springs, CO 80909
719-866-4618
teamusa.org/about-the-usopc/olympic-paralympic
-training-centers/csoptc/about

The US Olympic & Paralympic Training Center in Colorado Springs is home to several elite athletes, including gymnasts, who are training for future Olympic Games. Tours of the complex are sometimes available.

ABOUT THE AUTHOR

Brendan Flynn is a San Francisco resident and an author of numerous children's books.